Brown Bear
Starts School

Sue Tarsky

illustrated by
Marina Aizen

Albert Whitman & Company
Chicago, Illinois

It was Brown Bear's first day of school.

He was wearing his new sweater and his new scarf.

He was carrying his new book bag, with his new notebook in it, and his new pencil case, filled with his new pencils and erasers.

He even had his new lunch box, filled with his favorite lunch (a salmon sandwich and a small jar of honey). His mother had given him money to buy a small container of milk in the lunchroom.

Brown Bear was set. He was ready to go.

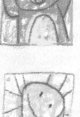

His father had kissed him goodbye before he left for work.

His brother had called out, "Good luck, Brown Bear. Catch you later!" as he ran out the door to the school bus the older kids took.

His mother was waiting by the door to walk him to school.

Brown Bear wasn't moving.

"What if they don't like me?" he asked.

"They will," she answered him. "You know most of the other kids in your class already, Brown Bear. You know Pinkie Piglet and Little Monkey and Big Bulldog and Long Crocodile and the Chicklet triplets, Chick, Chickie, and Chuck."

"What if I can't hear the teacher?" Brown Bear asked his mother.

"Can you hear me?" whispered his mother.

"Yes," he said.

Brown Bear's mother just looked at him.

"What if I'm not wearing the right clothes?" asked Brown Bear, with a little cough, so she wouldn't hear the frog that was stuck in his throat.

"Then we'll go shopping right after school and buy you new clothes," his mother told him, giving him a little hug.

"OK," said Brown Bear. "I guess I'm ready now."

Brown Bear and his mother walked out the front door and down the front path to the sidewalk.

"Hello, Brown Bear," said Pinkie Piglet's mother. She and Pinkie Piglet were walking to school too. Pinkie Piglet was wearing a sweater and a scarf and carrying a lunch box and a book bag.

"Hello, Mrs. Piglet," answered Brown Bear, politely.

"Well, hello, Brown Bear and Pinkie Piglet," said Little Monkey's father. He and Little Monkey were walking just behind them. Little Monkey was also wearing a sweater and a scarf and carrying a lunch box and a book bag.

"Hello, Mr. Monkey," answered Brown Bear and Pinkie Piglet, politely. The parents all smiled at each other.

They reached the school playground. Brown Bear could see his friend Big Bulldog playing on the swings and Long Crocodile and the Chicklet triplets, Chick, Chickie, and Chuck, tossing a ball to each other.

"Can we play too?" asked Brown Bear.

"Sure," said Long Crocodile.

Brown Bear, Pinkie Piglet, and Little Monkey joined their friends, and Chickie tossed the ball to Little Monkey.

"Look how far I can throw now!" said Little Monkey, and he threw the ball toward Chuck.

The ball flew right over Chuck's head and right over the playground fence.

It landed on the other side of the street, rolled a few feet, and stopped.

"I'm sorry!" said Little Monkey. "I didn't mean to throw it so hard. I'll go get it."

Brown Bear knew he wasn't allowed to cross the street and didn't think that Little Monkey was allowed to either. Brown Bear looked around to ask his mother what to do but couldn't see her.

"We aren't supposed to cross the street alone, Little Monkey," Brown Bear told him. "I'll go find Miss Zipper."

And just as he turned to look for her, he saw his mother with Mrs. Piglet and Mr. Monkey, coming toward them.

"Our ball went across the street," said Little Monkey. "I threw it too hard. Brown Bear told me not to go get it."

Mrs. Bear looked at Brown Bear and smiled. "You did the right thing, Brown Bear." She leaned down and whispered in his ear, "All by yourself."

Brown Bear smiled. He knew what to do!

"I'll get the ball," Mr. Monkey told them.

They all turned as Miss Zipper came up to them. She was holding someone's hand. "Hello, Brown Bear and Pinkie Piglet and Little Monkey. Welcome to Parker House School. This is Baby Bunny. It's her first day of school too. Her family has just moved here, and Baby Bunny doesn't know anyone."

"Would you like to play with us until the bell rings?"
Brown Bear asked Baby Bunny.

"Oh yes!" Baby Bunny smiled.

"I like your sweater and scarf," Brown Bear told her as they all walked toward the swings. "You can have half my salmon sandwich and some of my honey at lunchtime, if you like."

"I have an apple we can share," said Pinkie Piglet.

"And you can have some of my peanuts," said Little Monkey.

"Thank you," said Baby Bunny. "You can have some of my lettuce and carrots too. They're in a paper bag. My mother said she'd take me shopping right after school. I'll get a lunch box and a book bag."

"I was scared about starting school," Baby Bunny told them. "I don't have any friends here yet, and I didn't know if I would hear the teacher, and I didn't know if I had the right clothes."

"I was a little nervous too," said Brown Bear.

"Well, you can hear Miss Zipper," said Pinkie Piglet.

"Your clothes are just right," said Little Monkey.

"And we'll be your friends," said Brown Bear.

for Lisa, always
—ST

For all the children starting school: I hope you find great friends!
—MA

Library of Congress Cataloging-in-Publication data is on file with the publisher.

Text copyright © 2019 by Sue Tarsky
Illustrations copyright © 2019 by Albert Whitman & Company
Illustrated by Marina Aizen
First published in the United States of America in 2019 by Albert Whitman & Company
ISBN 978-0-8075-0773-5 (hardcover)
ISBN 978-0-8075-0771-1 (ebook)

Printed in China
10 9 8 7 6 5 4 3 2 1 WKT 24 23 22 21 20 19

Design by Rick DeMonico

For more information about Albert Whitman & Company,
visit our website at www.albertwhitman.com.

100 Years of Albert Whitman & Company
Celebrate with us in 2019!